Once-Upon-A-Time

Three Cat and Mouse Tales

Puss-in-Boots

Town Mouse and Country Mouse

Dick Whittington and His Cat

Retold by Marilyn Helmer • Illustrated by Josée Masse

Kids Can Press

For Misty, Star and Panda, and all the other felines who have left their pawprints in my heart. — M. H.

For Luc and Alice. — J. M.

Text © 2004 Marilyn Helmer
Illustrations © 2004 Josée Masse

Kids Can Press acknowledges the financial support of the Government of Ontario, through the Ontario Media Development Corporation's Ontario Book Initiative; the Ontario Arts Council; the Canada Council for the Arts; and the Government of Canada, through the BPIDP, for our publishing activity.

Published in Canada by
Kids Can Press Ltd.
29 Birch Avenue
Toronto, ON M4V 1E2

Published in the U.S. by
Kids Can Press Ltd.
2250 Military Road
Tonawanda, NY 14150

www.kidscanpress.com

The artwork in this book was rendered in acrylic.
The text is set in Berkeley.

Series Editor: Debbie Rogosin
Editor: David MacDonald
Design: Marie Bartholomew

Printed and bound in Hong Kong, China, by Book Art Inc., Toronto
This book is smyth sewn casebound.

CM 04 0 9 8 7 6 5 4 3 2 1

National Library of Canada Cataloguing in Publication Data

Helmer, Marilyn
   Three cat and mouse tales / retold by Marilyn Helmer ; illustrated by Josée Masse.
(Once-upon-a-time)
Contents: Puss-in-Boots — Town mouse and country mouse — Dick Whittington and his cat.
ISBN 1-55074-943-9

1. Fairy tales. I. Masse, Josée II. Title. III. Series: Helmer, Marilyn. Once-upon-a-time.

PS8565.E4594T42 2004   j398.2   C2003-903062-8
PZ7

Kids Can Press is a corus™ Entertainment company

Contents

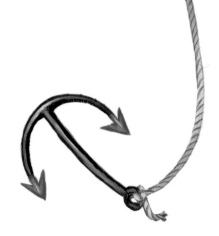

Puss-in-Boots

Many years ago there lived an old miller who had three sons. One day he called them together and said, "I have nothing to leave you except my mill, my donkey and my faithful cat, Puss. But you will each find your fortune if you use these gifts well."

When the old man died, the mill went to the eldest son, the donkey to the middle son, and Puss to Tom, the youngest. "My brothers may be able to make their fortunes with the mill and the donkey," Tom said to himself, "but who ever heard of making one's fortune with a cat?"

Now as everyone knows, cats are clever creatures, and Puss was cleverer than most. "If you give me a drawstring sack and a pair of boots," he said to Tom, "I will show you how to make your fortune."

"There may be more to this cat than meets the eye," Tom thought. He went right out and bought Puss a pair of red leather boots and a sturdy drawstring sack.

Puss was delighted. He quickly stepped into the boots and declared, "From now on I wish to be known as Puss-in-Boots." Then he picked up the sack, went to the meadow and caught a plump young rabbit. With the rabbit in the sack, he set off for the King's palace.

"Let me in," Puss told the guard at the palace gate. "My master has sent me with a gift for the King."

When the King heard there was a cat wearing red leather boots waiting to see him, he was quite intrigued. "Bring him to me at once," he ordered the guard.

In the throne room, Puss presented the rabbit to the King. "A gift from my master, the Marquis of Carabas," said Puss, inventing the name on the spot.

The King was very pleased, for rabbit pie was his favorite dish. "Be sure to thank your master for his gracious gift," he said.

From then on, Puss brought the King a present of fresh fish or game every day. Each time, he explained that the gift was from the Marquis of Carabas. Soon Puss-in-Boots became a court favorite, and the name of the Marquis of Carabas was on everyone's lips.

One day the King told Puss that he and his daughter were planning to go for a ride in the country. Puss rushed home to Tom and said, "We are about to make our fortune! Go to the riverbank, take off your clothes and jump into the water. I will take care of the rest."

Tom could make no sense of this, but he did as he was told. Puss hid Tom's ragged clothes behind a bilberry bush and waited for the King's coach.

A short while later, the royal coach came rumbling along, followed by two guards on horseback. Puss leapt out of the bushes. "Help! Help!" he cried. "My master, the Marquis of Carabas, has been robbed! Thieves have stolen his clothes and left him in the river."

The King immediately told his coachman to stop. "Save my good friend, the Marquis of Carabas!" he ordered the guards.

"Hurry, before he drowns," the Princess shouted.

The guards raced to the riverbank at a furious gallop. As soon as they had pulled Tom out of the water, the King sent his guards back to the palace to bring the finest set of clothes they could find.

Dressed in the King's clothes, Tom looked as noble as any marquis. Puss presented him to the King and the Princess. "The Marquis of Carabas at your service," said Puss.

The King was impressed. "Would you care to ride with us?" he asked.

"Please do," the Princess encouraged, for she was quite taken with handsome Tom.

"It would be my pleasure," Tom replied. With that he climbed into the coach and sat beside the Princess.

As the coach rumbled off down the road, Puss took a shortcut through some fields where workers were cutting grain. The fields belonged to a fierce ogre who lived in a nearby castle. But Puss warned the workers, "If the King asks whose fields these are, tell him they belong to the Marquis of Carabas. If you don't, I'll have you chopped into tiny pieces!" he added and off he ran.

When his coach passed by the fields, the King called to the workers, "What a fine crop you have there. Tell me, who owns this land?"

"The Marquis of Carabas, Your Majesty," the workers answered, for no one wanted to be chopped into tiny pieces.

"What a wealthy man he must be," the King thought, glancing at Tom with approval.

Meanwhile, Puss had arrived at the ogre's castle. He marched up to the door and knocked loudly.

The ogre was just about to sit down to an enormous feast. Furious at the interruption, he stomped to the door and yanked it open. "Who dares interrupt my dinner?" he snarled, glaring down at Puss.

Puss stood his ground. "I have heard that you have magical powers and can turn yourself into anything you wish," he said boldly. "But I don't believe a word of it."

"Just watch me," snapped the ogre. In the twitch of a whisker, he turned himself into a huge lion whose roars shook the castle walls.

"Quite impressive," said Puss, quickly jumping to the safety of a windowsill. "Of course it must be easy to turn into a creature as large as a lion. I'll bet you can't turn yourself into something small, like a mouse."

"Watch again," snarled the ogre and he changed himself into a tiny gray mouse. With a triumphant hiss, Puss pounced on the mouse and gobbled it up! That was the end of the ogre.

Now that the castle was his, Puss raced back to the road. When the King's coach drew near, he threw open the gates and cried, "Welcome to the home of the Marquis of Carabas!"

"All this land and a castle, too!" exclaimed the King. Tom just smiled graciously, for he was too surprised to speak. "My father was right," he said to himself. "I did indeed find my fortune with Puss!"

"I have prepared a feast for our honored guests," said Puss, bowing to the King and the Princess. He led everyone to the banquet hall, where the ogre's meal lay waiting. What a joyful feast it was! The King and Puss spent most of their time eating. But Tom and the Princess were so busy talking to each other, they scarcely touched their food.

And so it was that a poor miller's son named Tom became known as the Marquis of Carabas, and a clever cat named Puss became known as Puss-in-Boots. Not long after, Tom and the Princess were married, and they lived happily together for many a year. As for Puss, he never caught another mouse in his life. Instead he dined on salmon and cream and other delicacies most cats only dream of.

Town Mouse and Country Mouse

Once upon a time, a little Country Mouse lived in a hollow beneath the root of a great oak tree. Every morning at sunup, she ate her breakfast and tidied her cozy house. Then she scurried off to the woods to pick nuts and berries. Sometimes she stopped at the farmer's field to gather seeds and corn. When the shadows lengthened in late afternoon, Country Mouse hurried home and made her dinner. By twilight she was in bed, fast asleep.

One day she said to herself, "How nice it would be to have some company. I do believe I will invite my cousin Town Mouse to come for a visit." And so she did.

The day her cousin was to arrive, Country Mouse worked all morning cleaning the house. She prepared a fine lunch of wild onion stew, toasted barley seeds and crisp acorn cookies.

Then she set the table with her best bits of china and placed a bouquet of wildflowers in the center. "My dear little house has never looked lovelier," she said, standing back to admire her work. Finally Country Mouse put on her favorite cotton dress, and sat by the window to wait for her cousin.

Town Mouse came dressed in silk pants, a velvet jacket and shiny leather shoes. Country Mouse made him welcome and showed him around her house.

"Goodness, what a tiny place you have! My house is much larger than yours," he boasted.

"My house may be small, but it's very cozy," replied Country Mouse. "You must be hungry after your trip, Cousin. Let's have some lunch."

Country Mouse thoroughly enjoyed the meal she had worked so hard to prepare. But Town Mouse turned up his nose at everything.

"You've hardly eaten a bite!" exclaimed Country Mouse. "Aren't you hungry?"

"I'm used to much finer food than this," said Town Mouse. "Now tell me, Cousin, what do you do for excitement around here?"

"The farmer will be out on his wagon collecting hay," said Country Mouse. "Let's go for a ride and I'll show you the countryside."

They were scarcely settled in the wagon when Town Mouse began to complain. The hay made him sniffle and sneeze, and he didn't like the rough ride. "Too bumpy!" he squeaked. Afterward they went to the bramble patch to pick blackberries. Town Mouse grumbled about the hard work. "Too much trouble!" he squealed. When Country Mouse suggested a nap in the sun, Town Mouse rolled his eyes. "Dear Cousin," he said, "your country life is dull and boring. Come visit me in town. I'll show you how exciting life can be."

The next morning Town Mouse and Country Mouse set off together. When they reached the town, Country Mouse clapped her paws over her ears. "Never in my life have I heard so much noise!" she exclaimed, hurrying to keep up with her cousin. She trembled with fear as they dodged carts and buggies and stamping feet. By the time they came to the house where Town Mouse lived, Country Mouse was exhausted.

"You'll feel better when you've had something to eat," said Town Mouse. "Come along. You're in for a treat!"

As Country Mouse followed her cousin from room to room, her eyes grew wide at all she saw. There were thick carpets on the floors, silk drapes at the windows and fine furniture everywhere. Country Mouse had never seen anything so grand.

"This room is the best of all," said Town Mouse, leading her into the dining room. He scrambled up the leg of a huge table. Country Mouse scooted after him.

The table was laden with the remains of a delicious lunch. There were half-eaten rolls, leftover scalloped potatoes and one whole serving of ham-and-noodle casserole. A large platter held crackers and six different kinds of cheeses. Next to that was a bowl of rosy apples.

Country Mouse could hardly believe her eyes. "Is this all for us?" she gasped.

"If we're quick," said Town Mouse.

"What do you mean?" asked Country Mouse, but her cousin was already stuffing chunks of ham and cheese into his mouth.

Country Mouse was just about to nibble her first noodle when she heard the sound of footsteps approaching. In came a maid with a large tray. "Quick, hide!" squeaked Town Mouse.

The maid marched over to the table and began stacking dishes so quickly she almost scooped up the two mice. Town Mouse hid under a pile of crackers. Country Mouse cowered behind a vase.

When the maid left, Town Mouse poked his head out from among the crackers. "We're safe now," he said. But the words were hardly out of his mouth when two children raced into the room.

"Take cover!" squealed Town Mouse. He ducked behind the bowl of apples, pulling Country Mouse with him.

The children leaned across the table to help themselves to the apples. In their haste they knocked over the bowl. Apples rolled in all directions, and the mice barely managed to scramble to safety. Town Mouse squeezed under the rim of the platter. Country Mouse followed him, shaking from nose to tail.

Then suddenly, through an open window, leapt the biggest cat Country Mouse had ever seen.

"Run for your life!" screeched Town Mouse. He scurried across the table, jumped onto the floor and ducked into a hole by the fireplace. Country Mouse darted after him. As she reached the hole, the cat's huge paw came down on her tail. Town Mouse grabbed his cousin and pulled her to safety, just in the nick of time. Country Mouse collapsed on the floor, trembling all over.

"Now that you've seen how exciting town life is," said Town Mouse, "don't you agree that country life is dull and boring?"

"It might be dull and boring to you," exclaimed Country Mouse, "but the peace and quiet suit me just fine!"

With that, Country Mouse said good-bye to her cousin. Quick as the flick of a tail, she was out the door and on her way. By sunset, she was back in her cozy home beneath the great oak tree.

From that day to this, Town Mouse has never been seen in the country and Country Mouse has never been seen in the town.

Town or country, east or west,
The home you love is the home that's best!

Dick Whittington and His Cat

Long ago in England, there lived an orphan boy named Dick Whittington. With no one to care for him, Dick roamed the countryside, finding food and shelter wherever he could. He often chatted with travelers he met along the way, fascinated by their stories of the places they had been. Above all, Dick loved to hear tales about the great city of London.

"There's no finer place in the world," one man told him. "The streets are paved with gold!"

"And plenty of food for all," said another.

One day, Dick met a wagoner who was heading for London. "Why don't you come along with me?" the man suggested.

"Indeed I will," said Dick, for he was eager to see the great city for himself. He quickly jumped onto the wagon and the two set off on the long journey.

Days later the weary pair finally arrived at London Bridge. Across the River Thames lay the bustling city. Dick was so excited he could hardly speak. But when they reached the city, he stared in dismay. Instead of streets paved with gold, all he saw were dirty cobblestones, grimy buildings and crowds of people.

"I must leave you now," said the wagoner. "Good-bye and good luck, my lad."

Dick waved good-bye and then set out to explore the city.

All day long he searched
in vain for the streets of
gold. No one spoke to
Dick or even looked
his way. Finally, tired
and discouraged, he fell
asleep in the doorway of a
great stone house.

The next morning the cook found
him sleeping there. "Off you go!" she shouted, with a thump of her
broom on his backside. "There'll be no beggar boys on the Fitzwarrens'
doorstep."

Dick scrambled to his feet, trying to dodge the flailing broom. Just
then, Mr. Fitzwarren and his daughter, Alice, rushed out to see what
was going on.

"Cook, stop that at once!" cried Alice, as the broom again descended
on poor Dick.

"What are you doing here, young lad?" asked Mr. Fitzwarren. Dick quickly told them his story.

"Couldn't we give him a job working for us?" Alice asked her father.

"That's a fine idea!" Mr. Fitzwarren exclaimed. "Cook could use a helper," he said to Dick. "In return, she will see that you have plenty to eat and a place to sleep."

"I'd be happy to work for you," Dick said gratefully. He thought that Mr. Fitzwarren and his daughter were two of the kindest people he had ever met.

Alas, Cook was another story. She made Dick sleep in the drafty attic, which was overrun with rats and mice. When the Fitzwarrens were not around, she delighted in giving him the dirtiest jobs she could find. And for supper every night, Cook just shoved a small bowl of cold pot-scrapings in front of him. But Dick never complained.

Not long afterward, Dick ran into his first bit of good fortune. A woman at the market gave him a penny for carrying her packages. Near one of the stalls, Dick noticed a girl playing with a pretty gray kitten. The girl was happy to sell the kitten for a penny, so Dick traded his good fortune for better. He named the kitten Lady Puss, and before long she had rid the attic of rats and mice. In return, Dick shared his pot-scrapings and a corner of his ragged blanket with her.

As time passed, Dick settled quite contentedly into his life in London. Mr. Fitzwarren praised his work and told Dick that he was growing into a fine young man. Alice often stopped by the kitchen to chat with him, and he became very fond of her. With that and his friend Lady Puss, Dick managed to put up with Cook's bad temper.

Then one day Mr. Fitzwarren called his staff together. "I'm sending a ship to faraway lands on a trading voyage," he said. "If you have goods to trade, you may send them along."

The other servants rushed off to collect their baubles and trinkets, but Dick stayed behind. "Have you nothing to send?" asked Alice.

"All I have in the world is my cat, Lady Puss," Dick answered.

"Then you must send her," said Mr. Fitzwarren.

"Not Lady Puss!" Alice exclaimed, for she knew how much Dick loved his cat. "I will give him my silver locket to send instead."

"Dick must send something of his own," said Mr. Fitzwarren. He turned to Dick. "Lady Puss is just the thing, for she is an excellent mouser. And who knows what treasures you may get in exchange?"

Reluctantly Dick went to the attic and returned with Lady Puss. After one last fond pat, he handed her to Mr. Fitzwarren.

With Lady Puss gone, the attic was once again overrun with rats and mice. Cook made Dick work harder than ever. She mocked him for sending his beloved cat to sea. "What do you think that worthless creature will fetch?" she sneered. Finally, unable to stand her cruelty any longer, Dick decided to run away.

One morning before sunup, he tiptoed out the door and headed back toward the River Thames. As he crossed over London Bridge, Dick turned to take one last look at the city. Just then, the bells of Bow Church rang out. Dick had often heard the Bow Bells, but this time the ringing sounded like words, speaking directly to him:

Turn again, Whittington,
Lord Mayor of London.

"Me? Lord Mayor of London?" Dick gasped. "Could that ever come true?" There was only one way to find out. He turned, hurried back to the Fitzwarrens' house and was at work in the kitchen before Cook knew he'd been gone.

Meanwhile, Lady Puss was having an adventure of her own. A violent storm had washed the ship ashore at a Moorish city on the coast of Barbary.

The Moors welcomed the ship's arrival, for they were eager to see what treasures and trinkets the sailors had brought to trade. At the royal palace, the King threw a lavish banquet in honor of his guests. The sailors watched, wide-eyed, as servants brought in dish after dish of exotic food and placed it before them. But just as the feast was about to begin, hordes of mice poured into the banquet room. They scrambled onto the table and began to gobble up everything in sight!

While the servants tried in vain to chase the mice away, the royal couple stood by, helplessly wringing their hands.

"Every meal is spoiled by these horrid creatures!" cried the King.

"If only we could be rid of them," sobbed the Queen.

"Have you no cats?" asked the captain.

"Cats?" exclaimed the King, looking puzzled. "What is a cat?" At that time, cats were unknown in the land of the Moors.

"When it comes to dealing with mice, a cat is the most wonderful creature in the world," said the captain. He immediately sent someone to fetch Lady Puss. The minute she was turned loose, she prowled and pounced until there wasn't a single mouse left in the palace.

The king was so grateful to be rid of the mice that he bought the ship's entire cargo. In exchange for Lady Puss, he offered a chest overflowing with jewels.

After the ship returned to London, Mr. Fitzwarren presented Dick with the chest of jewels. Dick could hardly believe his eyes. "Is all this mine?" he gasped.

"Indeed it is," Mr. Fitzwarren assured him. "You are a very wealthy young man." To the rest of the household he declared, "From now on, Dick will be known as *Mister* Whittington."

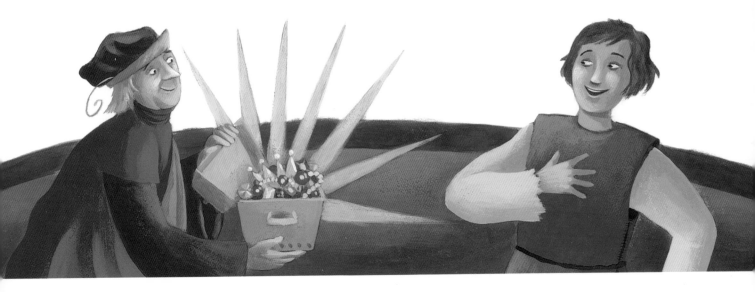

But Dick did not keep all the treasure for himself. Although Mr. Fitzwarren and Alice would not accept a penny from him, Dick generously rewarded the captain and crew for taking care of Lady Puss. He also gave presents to the other servants and even to Cook, in spite of her cruelty to him.

Soon after, to Mr. Fitzwarren's delight, Dick asked Alice to be his wife. She accepted happily, for she had grown to love Dick as much as he loved her.

Some people would have put on airs with such newfound wealth. But not Dick Whittington. Whenever he saw someone in need, he gave with a generous heart.

King Henry the Fifth heard the story of the young orphan boy who had risen from beggar to gentleman, and decided to make him a knight. So Dick became Sir Richard Whittington, and he was elected Lord Mayor of London not once, not twice, but three times. Indeed the Bow Bells had spoken the truth when they rang out:

> *Turn again, Whittington,*
> *Lord Mayor of London.*

And if that news doesn't please you, I don't know what will!